WALT DISNEY's
Winnie the Pooh
The Blustery Day

A Story by A. A. Milne

A GOLDEN BOOK · NEW YORK

Western Publishing Company, Inc.,
Racine, Wisconsin 53404

One Blustery day, Winnie-the-Pooh decided to visit his Thoughtful Spot. He sat down and was just saying, "Think, think, think, think," to himself, when Gopher popped up beside him.

"What's wrong, Sonny?" Gopher asked Pooh. "Don't you like Windsdays?"

"Oh, is that what today is?" Pooh said, surprised. "Then I think I shall wish everyone a Happy Windsday. And I shall begin with my Very Dear Friend, Piglet."

And Piglet, being the Very Dear Friend he was, thought he would go with Winnie-the-Pooh on the rest of his rounds.

They went to Pooh's house first, and since it was nearly eleven o'clock, Pooh asked Piglet in, out of the wind, and they had a Little Something.

Then they went on to Kanga's house, holding on to each other and shouting, "Isn't it?" and "What?" and "I can't hear." By the time they got to Kanga's house, they were so buffeted that they stayed to Lunch.

As they went from Kanga's house to Rabbit's (where they had a Little More) to Christopher Robin's (where they had a Very Nearly tea) to Eeyore's (where they didn't have Anything at All), the day got Blustier and Blustier.

Pooh and Piglet were quite blown out when they reached Owl's house.

"Sit down, Pooh. Sit down, Piglet," said Owl kindly. "Make yourselves comfortable. Correct me if I am wrong," he added, "but am I right in supposing that it is a very Blusterous day outside?"

"Very," said Piglet, who was quietly thawing his ears and wishing that he was safely back in his own house.

"I thought so," said Owl. "It was on just such a Blusterous day as this that my Uncle Robert—a portrait of whom you see upon the wall on your right, Piglet—while returning in the late forenoon from a—What's that?"

There was a loud cracking noise.

Pooh's side of the room slowly tilted upward, floor and all.

Uncle Robert's portrait met Piglet's chair just as Piglet was leaving it.

There was another loud crack. Owl's room collected itself—and there was silence all around.

"Pooh," said Owl severely, "did *you* do that?"

"No," said Pooh humbly. "I don't *think* I did."

"Then who did?"

"I think it was the wind," said Piglet. "I think your house has blown down."

And, sure enough, it had.

As soon as the wind died down, Eeyore and Christopher Robin came by to see how much damage had been done.

"If you ask me," Eeyore said, shaking his head, "when a house looks like that, it's time to find another one."

"That's a very good idea, Eeyore," said Christopher Robin.

"It might take a day or two," Eeyore went on, "but I'll find a new one for him. He noticed me the other day, you know. A kind fellow, Owl."

So Eeyore went stumping about the Hundred Acre Wood in search of a new home for Owl. Each house he found seemed to have Some Little Thing Wrong with it—

—like the one he saw right where the Stream became the River.

"There's one. Cozy cottage. Nice location. Bit damp for Owl, though."

Christopher Robin was giving a party for Winnie-the-Pooh when Eeyore announced, at last, "I found it. Owl's new home. If you will come with me, I will show it to you."

In a little while, they came to the house which Eeyore had found, but for some minutes before they came to it, Piglet was nudging Pooh, and Pooh was nudging Piglet, and they were saying, "It is!" and "It can't be!" and "It is, *really!*" to each other.

And when they got there, it really was.
"There!" said Eeyore proudly, stopping
them outside Piglet's house. "Just the
house for Owl. Don't you think so, Piglet?"

And then Piglet did a Noble Thing. "Yes, it's just the house for Owl," he said grandly. "And I hope he'll be very happy in it." Then Piglet gulped twice, because he had been very happy in it himself.

Christopher Robin was proud of Piglet,
but he wondered what his friend would do
now. "What would *you* do, Piglet, if *your*
house were blown down?" he asked.

Before Piglet could think, Pooh answered
for him. "He'd come and live with me."

Piglet squeezed Pooh's paw. "Thank you,
Pooh," he said, "I should love to."